# The Great White
# Man-Eating Shark

ISBN 0-590-98740-2

Text copyright © 1989 by Margaret Mahy.
Illustrations copyright © 1989 by Jonathan Allen.
All rights reserved. Published by Scholastic Inc., 555 Broadway, New York, NY 10012, by arrangement with Dial Books for Young Readers, a division of Penguin Books USA Inc. TRUMPET and the TRUMPET logo are registered trademarks of Scholastic Inc.

12 11 10 9 8 7 6 5 4 3 2 1          6 7 8 9/9 0 1/0

Printed in the U.S.A.

# Margaret Mahy

# The Great White Man-Eating Shark

*– a Cautionary Tale –*

pictures by Jonathan Allen

There was once a boy called Norvin who was a good actor but rather plain. In fact, he looked very like a shark. He had small sharkish eyes, a pointed sharkish head, and sharp sharkish teeth.

Unfortunately, there are not many plays written with good parts for sharks, so Norvin took up swimming instead. He soon became a good swimmer and learned to shoot through the water like a silver arrow.

Norvin lived near a wonderful beach called Caramel Cove, but he had to share it with lots of other swimmers. When Norvin tried shooting through the water like a silver arrow, the other swimmers got in his way. This made him cross and resentful.

What's the use of being able to shoot through the water like a silver arrow if everyone gets in my way? he thought. So he came up with a wicked plan.

Out of plastic he made himself the dorsal fin of a great white man-eating shark. Then he strolled around the headland, thought a few sharkish thoughts, strapped it on, and slid into the clear blue water.

Mrs. Scorpio, who ran the bakery, was bobbing harmlessly up and down in the waves when suddenly she saw the dorsal fin of a great white man-eating shark heading straight for her.

If you are swimming and see a great white man-eating shark heading straight for you, the thing to do is to leave the water in a quiet and dignified way. But Mrs. Scorpio did not know this.

"Shark! Shark!" she yelled and flung herself onto the sand, screaming and kicking with terror.

What a panic there was! Up and down Caramel Cove people grabbed up their children, their dogs, and inflatable canoes. Within moments the sand was crowded with dripping bodies and the sea was completely empty. Everyone stared despairingly at the cruising dorsal fin. Many people thought they could just make out the shape of a great white man-eating shark cutting through the water beneath it. Norvin wore the expression a great white man-eating shark always wears when it is hungry, and his acting was so good, that even when he came up to breathe, people were convinced he was actually looking for prey.

It was a very hot day, but nobody dared go swimming again. Norvin had the whole of Caramel Cove to himself. He spent all afternoon shooting backwards and forwards like a silver arrow.

Everyone else watched enviously, sighing and rubbing suntan lotion onto one another. No one dared to share the sea with a great white man-eating shark. At last, Norvin swam out around the headland and vanished from sight.

After that, everyone except Norvin was too scared to go swimming at Caramel Cove.

"Norvin! Come out at once," his friends all cried. "There is a great white man-eating shark hanging around these parts."

Norvin laughed.

"Nonsense!" he said. "It is probably only a whale shark, or even a basking shark . . . and they are vegetarians, you know."

Norvin had the entire beach to himself for three whole days.

However, soon a few brave people, tired of seeing Norvin shooting to and fro like a silver arrow, started swimming again. Others joined them, and soon everyone was splashing around happily once more, enjoying the swimming and the summer.

But Norvin had grown used to having the beach to himself. He strolled around the headland, put on his dorsal fin, and swam back into Caramel Cove.

Mr. Dorsey, the plumber, was showing his little boy, Courtney, how to stand on his head in the water – something a plumber sometimes has to do. Suddenly, he found himself nose to nose with Norvin. He did not recognize Norvin, of course. He thought he was nose to nose with a great white man-eating shark.

If you find yourself nose to nose with a shark, the thing to do is to leave the water quietly – just as if your only thought was to rub in more suntan lotion. Mr. Dorsey did not know this.

"Shark! Shark!" he yelled. Grabbing up Courtney, he flung himself onto the sand, kicking and screaming in terror.

Within minutes Norvin had the beach all to himself once more. No one dared go swimming for a week at Caramel Cove ... no one except Norvin, that is. He shot to and fro like a silver arrow, while others watched longingly from the beach. Soon they could stand it no longer. A few brave people decided to take a risk, and Caramel Cove was once more splashing and bubbling with happy swimmers.

Norvin, however, was becoming greedy. He wanted Caramel Cove all to himself, all the time. So he strolled around the headland and put on his dorsal fin once more. Then he swam back to Caramel Cove, laughing to himself as he thought of all the terror he would cause.

But, suddenly, he felt he was not alone. Someone was swimming beside him. Who could it be? He looked out of the corner of his eye.

There, nuzzling up to him, was a great white man-eating shark – a female. Norvin was such a good actor that she did not realize he was merely pretending to be a shark. She gave him a very loving glance.

"You are the shark of my dreams," she said. "Marry me at once or I shall lose my temper and bite you!"

He shot like a silver arrow, dorsal fin and all, toward the beach and flung himself onto the sand where he lay, kicking and screaming with terror. Everyone could see at a glance just what Norvin had been up to.

The people of Caramel Cove put up a shark net across the mouth of the bay, but for the rest of the summer Norvin sat on the beach, watching other swimmers shoot backwards and forwards like silver arrows. He had had such a terrible shock that – shark net or not – he was too frightened to go swimming for a long, long time. Though he was a plain boy, he had made rather a good-looking shark, and I think he was very wise not to take any dangerous chances.